Professor Frank Mouse lived alone,
in a shed. He liked to collect
and make and mend
things.

He was

very

clever.

Frank could make or mend
almost anything from
the things he
collected.

One day, when
Frank was
wondering what
to make next,

he gazed out of
the shed window
and saw that all kinds
of other creatures
were collecting,

making

and mending things too.

When he saw how happy they were, all working together, he *longed* to join in but he was too shy.

"They have their friends to help them," he thought. "They do not need me."

That night Frank had
a brilliant idea!

He set to work

collecting,

watching,

reading

and sewing,

until at last he was finished.

Frank had made himself

his very own . . .

FRIEND!

Frank found his new friend, Teddy, very handy

and Teddy was keen to help.

Teddy tried to join
in, but it wasn't
always easy.

So one day, when Frank was out collecting,
Teddy decided to try and make
something by himself

as a surprise for when
his friend got home.

But instead of building things,

he
BROKE
them . . .

And instead of
mending things,

he
MUCKED
them up.

In fact the only
thing that
Teddy managed
to make was . . .

A MESS!

Frank *was* surprised when he got home.

He was also *very* angry

and he sent Teddy
out into the garden to
think about what he'd done.

Then he set about
mending everything
that had been broken.

As he worked, he couldn't
help thinking about
Teddy, outside
all alone . . .

But Teddy was not alone.

He was picking flowers for the bees
so they didn't have to fly so far
to collect their
pollen.

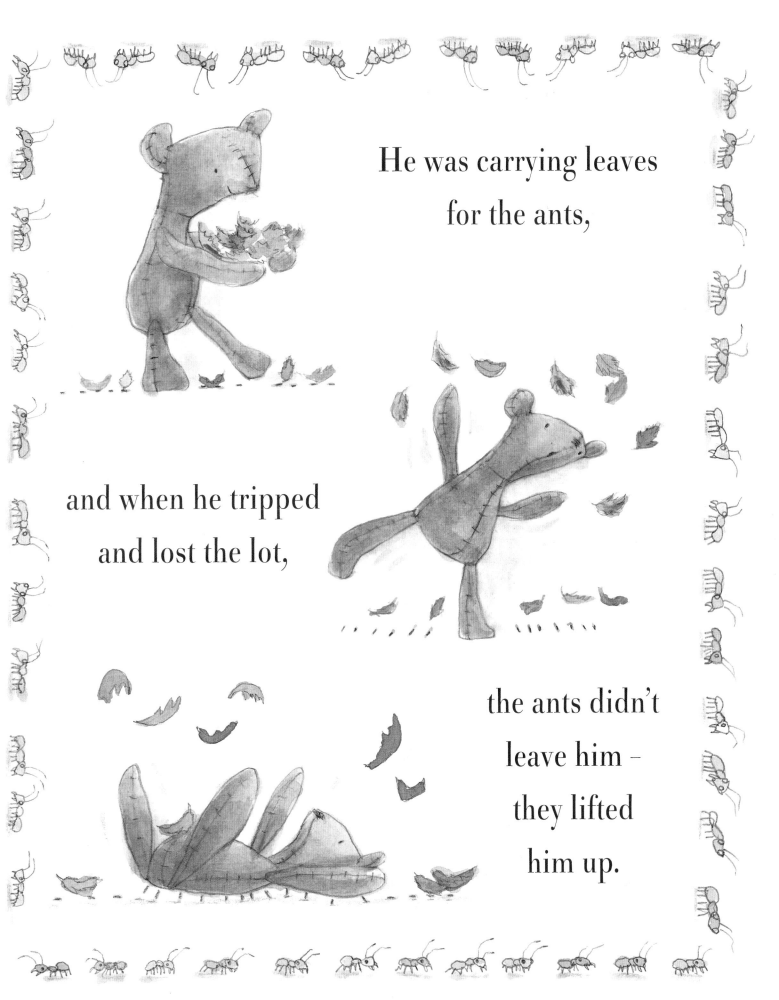

He was carrying leaves
for the ants,

and when he tripped
and lost the lot,

the ants didn't
leave him –
they lifted
him up.

Frank watched
as Teddy
brought twigs
for the birds
and they
taught him
how to make
a nest.

Teddy climbed
higher and
higher . . .

and when he lost his
grip and slipped,

Frank RAN and . . .

CAUGHT HIM

just in time!

From then on, Frank and Teddy
made many things together,
including

LOTS OF

FRIENDS.

For Peter and his teddy, and in memory
of its maker: A. E. Yates

FRANK AND TEDDY MAKE FRIENDS
A RED FOX BOOK 978 1 862 30864 0

First published in Great Britain by Jonathan Cape,
an imprint of Random House Children's Books
A Random House Group Company

Jonathan Cape edition published 2011
Red Fox edition published 2011

1 3 5 7 9 10 8 6 4 2

Copyright © Louise Yates, 2011

Red Fox Books are published by Random House Children's Books,
61-63 Uxbridge Road, London W5 5SA

www.**kidsatrandomhouse**.co.uk
www.**rbooks**.co.uk

Addresses for companies within The Random House Group Limited can be found at:
www.randomhouse.co.uk/offices.htm

THE RANDOM HOUSE GROUP Limited Reg. No. 954009

A CIP catalogue record for this book is available from the British Library.

Printed in China